Tweenies™

The Wobbly Jelly Hunt

CBeebies
BBC

One day, the Tweenies wanted to make
something that they all liked to eat.
   "Oh, can we make jelly?" asked Fizz. "I like jelly."
   "Me too," agreed Milo.
   "That's a good idea," said
Max. "You can each have
a different flavour. And
we can add some fruit,
too. I've got raspberries,
strawberries, oranges
and blackcurrants."
   "Mmmm. Fruit jellies!
I like the sound of
those," said Jake,
excitedly. The
Tweenies couldn't
wait to start.

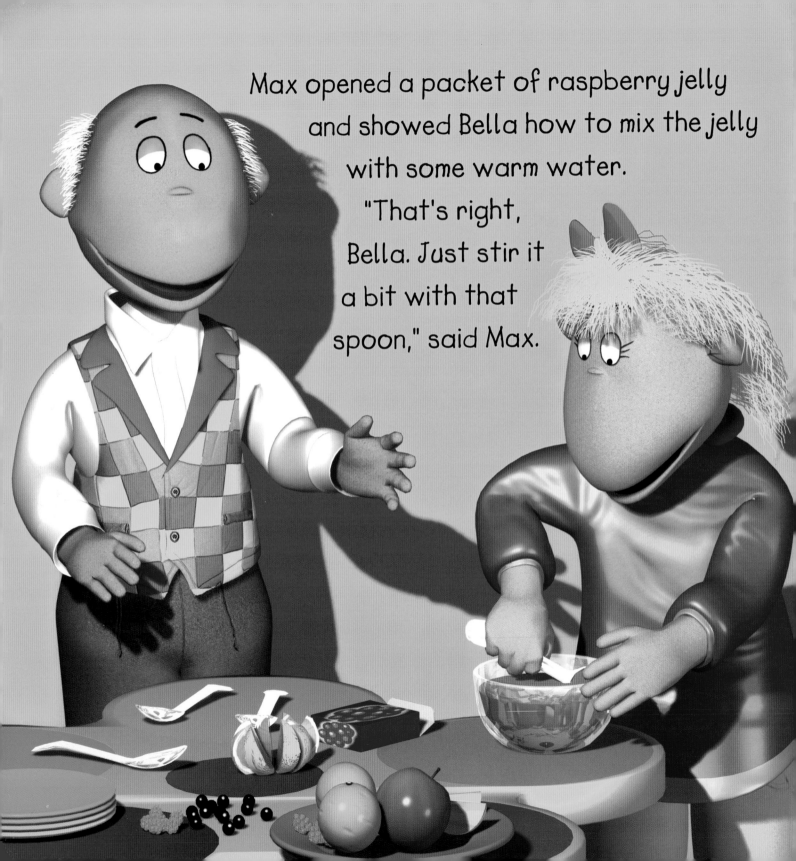

Max opened a packet of raspberry jelly and showed Bella how to mix the jelly with some warm water.
"That's right, Bella. Just stir it a bit with that spoon," said Max.

"What shall I do, Max?" asked Jake.

"Choose a flavour, Jake, and I'll show you how to make your jelly."

Jake chose strawberry and mixed the jelly with water, just like Bella had done.

"Oh, can I have orange flavour?" asked Fizz, excitedly.

"I suppose I'll have to have the blackcurrant then, because it's the only one left," said Milo.

Soon, the Tweenies were ready to pour the jellies into their moulds.

"Now we can add the fruit," said Max.

Bella added some raspberries to her jelly. Jake added some strawberries to his. Fizz put orange segments in her jelly and Milo sprinkled lots of blackcurrants into his.

Then Max put the jellies in the fridge.

"Mmmm, I'm hungry. Can we eat the jellies now?" asked Fizz.

"We've got to let them set first," said Max.

"But I want to taste one now!"
said Bella, crossly.

"Me, too!" said Milo
and Jake at the
same time.

Max explained that the jellies would be soft if they tried to eat them now.

"Jelly should be wobbly, not runny," said Max.

The Tweenies looked very disappointed.

"I can't wait much longer," said Jake, rubbing his tummy.

"Neither can I," agreed Bella.

"Nor me," said Fizz.

"What can we do while we're waiting?" asked Milo with a sigh.

Then Max had an idea.

"I know," he said. "You can go on a treasure hunt!"

Max explained.

"I'm going to give you some clues and you have to find the treasure," he said with a smile.

"That sounds like fun, Max," said Fizz. "Maybe we'll find gold and jewels."

"Let's get ready!" said Milo, and the Tweenies took off their overalls while Max prepared the first clue.

Max put some big paper circles on the floor in the middle of the playroom.

"These are stepping stones," explained Max.
"You have to jump on them to cross the alligator swamp, to find the first clue.
Careful – the alligators are hungry today!"

Fizz squealed as she jumped onto the first
stepping stone. Milo, Bella and Jake followed.
 "Ow – I think something bit me,"
shouted Jake.

"It's all right, Jake. There aren't any
real alligators," whispered Bella.
The stepping stones led into
the garden.

Max told them the first clue.

"I'm very colourful and you can climb up my steps to the top. The fun bit is when you whizz down again to the bottom. What am I?"

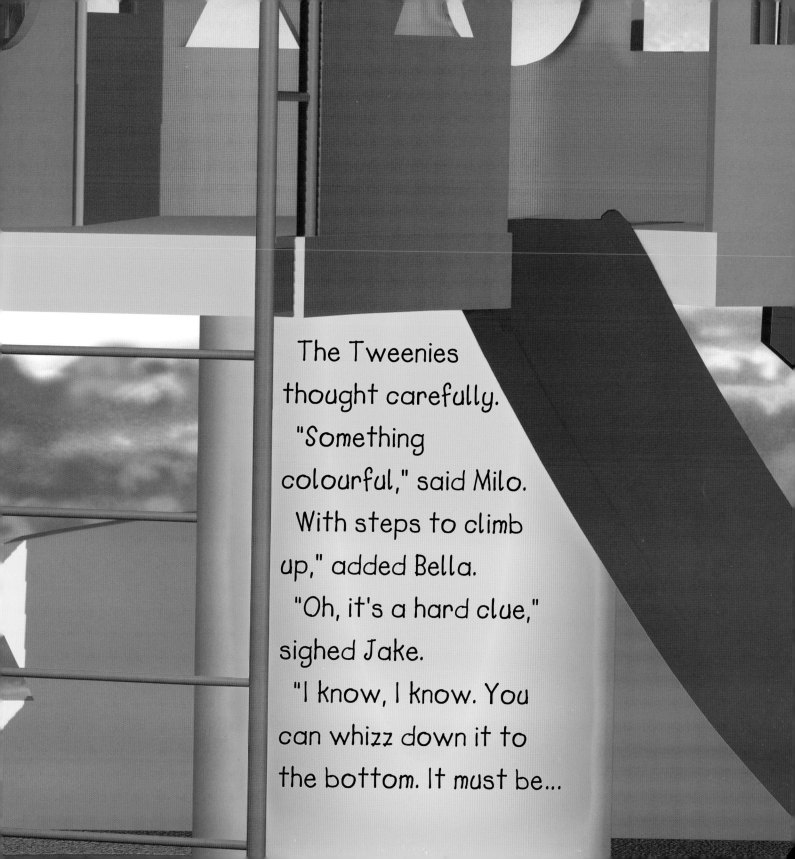

The Tweenies
thought carefully.
"Something
colourful," said Milo.
With steps to climb
up," added Bella.
"Oh, it's a hard clue,"
sighed Jake.
"I know, I know. You
can whizz down it to
the bottom. It must be...

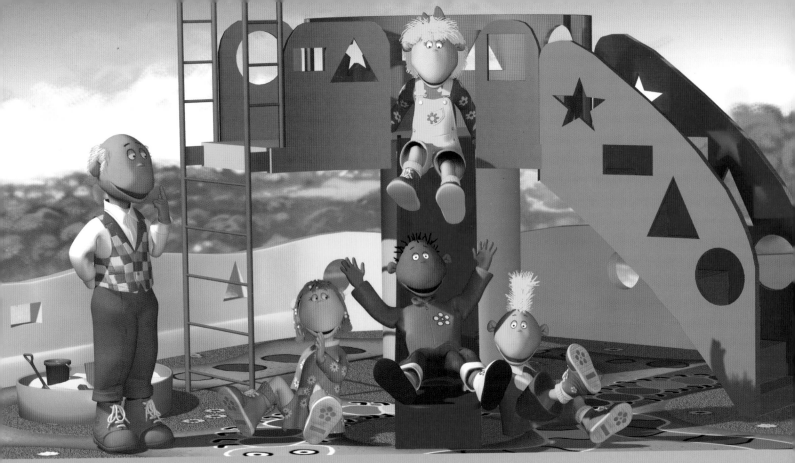

...the slide on the climbing frame!" cried Fizz.

One by one, theTweenies climbed up the steps of the climbing frame and whizzed down the slide, landing in a big heap at the bottom.

"What's the next clue, Max?" asked Milo, impatiently.

"Well," Max began. "The pink princess has been locked away at the top of the Green Tower. You have to rescue her and take her to the furry king and queen," he said, mysteriously.

"I know who the furry king and queen are," said Jake at once, spying Doodles and Izzles in a corner of the garden.

"But where's the Green Tower?" asked Fizz.

"It must be somewhere high up," decided Milo.

"Maybe the Green Tower is a...

...tree," said Bella, pointing.
The Tweenies looked up.
There, high up in one of the
trees, was a little pink doll,
wearing a pretty princess dress.

"That must be the pink princess," said Bella.

"But how are we going to rescue her? It's so high up," wailed Jake.

"Why not try working together?" suggested Max with a helpful wink.

"I've got an idea," said Fizz. "Jake's not very heavy. Milo can give him a piggy back and then he can reach up and grab the dolly, I mean the pink princess."

So Milo crouched down and Jake jumped up on his back.
"Hold on tight," said Milo.
"Ooooh, I feel a bit wobbly," said Jake.

Jake reached up as high as he could. At first he couldn't quite reach the doll, but with one last big stretch, he grabbed her and then handed her to Doodles and Izzles.

"Well done," said Max. "Are you ready for your next clue, now?"

"Oh, yes," said the Tweenies, all at once.

"Well, the next one's indoors. A very important picture was broken up into little pieces by a nasty goblin. You have to put it together again."

"Lots of little pieces?" wondered Bella.

"That make a picture?" thought Milo.

"I know," said Jake, spying a box on the floor. "It's this jigsaw puzzle."

"Hey, well done, Jakey," laughed Fizz.

They set to work and soon they had put all the pieces together. It was a picture of a house.

"Where's Max?" said Bella. "We need the next clue now."

"Maybe the house is a clue," said Milo, slowly.

The Tweenies looked up and there in the window of the playhouse were Doodles and Izzles, barking excitedly.

The Tweenies ran into the playhouse and...

...there was Max with the jellies.

"You've found your treasure," Max said.

"The fruit jellies are ready now," said Jake.

"Look, they're all wobbly!" laughed Milo.

"That was quick," said Fizz.

"Time passed quickly because we were enjoying ourselves," said Bella.

"Mmmm, I like treasure hunts," said Jake.

"Woof! So do we," said Doodles and Izzles.

THE END